For Sarah O, with thanks

First published in Great Britain in 2009 by Bloomsbury Publishing Plc.
Published in the United States of America in 2009 by Walker Publishing Company, Inc.
Visit Walker & Company's Web site at www.walkeryoungreaders.com

For information about permission to reproduce selections from this book, write to Permissions,
Walker & Company, 175 Fifth Avenue, New York, New York 10010

Library of Congress Cataloging-in-Publication Data
Foreman, Michael.
The littlest dinosaur's big adventure / written and illustrated by Michael Foreman.
p.   cm.
Summary: The littlest dinosaur discovers the advantages of being small as he frolics among the lily pads
with his new frog friends, and then bravely finds his way home after getting lost in the woods.
ISBN-13: 978-0-8027-9545-8 • ISBN-10: 0-8027-9545-5 (hardcover : alk. paper)
[1. Dinosaurs—Fiction. 2. Size—Fiction. 3. Lost children—Fiction.] I. Title.
PZ7.F7583Lk 2009   [E]—dc22   2008040297

Typeset in Goudy Old Style
Art created with watercolor and ink

Printed in China
2 4 6 8 10 9 7 5 3

All papers used by Walker & Company are natural, recyclable products
made from wood grown in well-managed forests. The manufacturing processes
conform to the environmental regulations of the country of origin.

The Littlest
DINOSAUR'S
BiG ADVENTURE

MiCHAEL FOREMAN

Walker & Company • New York

One day, the littlest dinosaur was sitting by the river and dangling his toes among the water lilies.

Suddenly a frog landed on a lily pad
next to the littlest dinosaur's feet.

Plip!

Plop!

Flip!

Flop!

The frog hopped to another lily pad and looked back at the littlest dinosaur. Then he hopped to the next lily pad and the next and looked back at him again.

Carefully, the littlest dinosaur stepped onto the nearest lily pad. It wibbled and wobbled but didn't sink. Then he stepped onto the next lily pad. When the frog saw that the littlest dinosaur was following him,

he did a double backflip and clapped his hands!

The littlest dinosaur was suddenly surrounded by frogs,
all somersaulting, hopping, and diving among the lilies.

"This is fun!" cried the littlest dinosaur. "At last I have some friends my own size." He followed the frogs, pad by pad, across the river.

Splish!

Splash!

When he reached the opposite riverbank, there were wild flowers that stretched as far as he could see. Here there were no big, clumsy dinosaurs to trample them—only bees buzzing and butterflies flitting from flower to flower.

A butterfly landed on the littlest dinosaur's nose and opened its wings.

"How lovely you are," whispered the littlest dinosaur, and he kept walking, surrounded by a cloud of beautiful butterflies.

"It's so much fun being small," he thought to himself. As he followed the butterflies, they flitted from one sunny spot to the next.

But soon there was no more sunlight. The butterflies were gone. There was nothing but dark forest.

"Oh, no," thought the littlest dinosaur. "It's not fun being small in the dark. But I have the heart of a dinosaur, so I can be brave. If I walk back the way I came, I will find my way out of here."

But from which way had he come? He had run all over
while following the butterflies and had lost his sense of
direction.

The littlest dinosaur looked around. Every tree looked
the same—dark and spooky. The littlest dinosaur was
frightened. Birds and bats flew squawking into the sky.
Eyes watched from behind trees.

The littlest dinosaur ran. He tripped and slipped and stumbled through the dark forest until he was so tired he could run no farther.

He crawled under the roots of a giant tree and was just reminding himself that, with the heart of a dinosaur, he shouldn't cry, when he heard sobbing nearby. Looking around the back of the tree, the littlest dinosaur saw the strangest little creature he had ever seen.

"I am lost,"
cried the little
creature.

"Don't cry," the littlest dinosaur replied.
"We'll be all right, you'll see."
He put his arm around the little creature and
together they walked through the forest until
the trees thinned and they could see the sky.

Suddenly it got very dark again and a big, terrifying shape swooped across the sky.

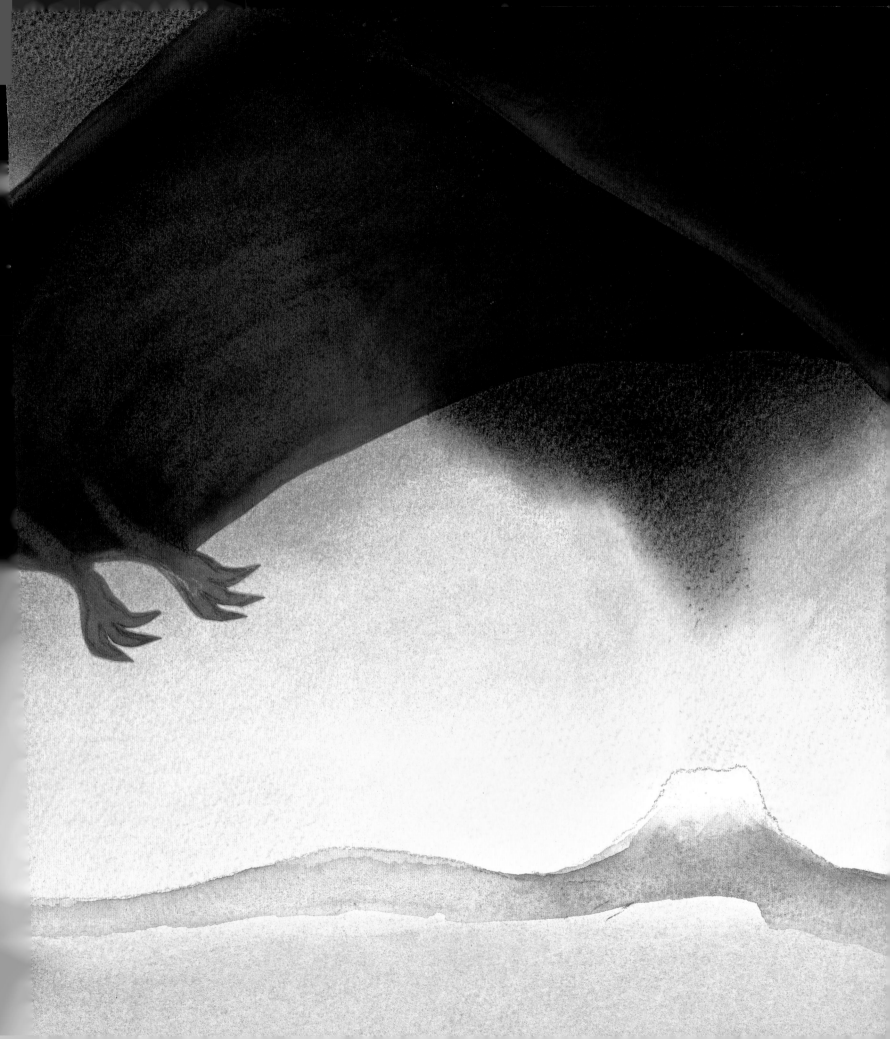

"Mommy!" cried the strange little creature. "Mommy!"
The little creature's mommy landed with a crash and folded
her great wings around her baby. Then she looked at the
littlest dinosaur. His knees trembled and his heart thumped.

"Come," the huge mommy said. "Let's get you home."

With her baby and the littlest dinosaur clinging to her neck,
she beat her great wings and soared over the forest.
The littlest dinosaur pointed to the far river.

Soon they were circling over the amazed faces
of the littlest dinosaur's family, who were all
very happy to see him.